Not Fair, Won't Share!

A Pinky and Blue Story

by Lindsey Gardiner

BARRON'S

For Corrie

First edition for the United States, its territories
and dependencies, Canada, and the Philippine Republic,
published 2002 by Barron's Educational Series, Inc.

First published in Great Britain in 2001 by Orchard Books, London

All inquiries should be addressed to:
Barron's Educational Series, Inc.
250 Wireless Boulevard
Hauppauge, New York 11788
http://www.barronseduc.com

Library of Congress Catalog Card No. 2001099432
International Standard Book No. 0-7641-2262-2

Printed in Hong Kong
9 8 7 6 5 4 3 2 1

Meet Pinky and Blue.

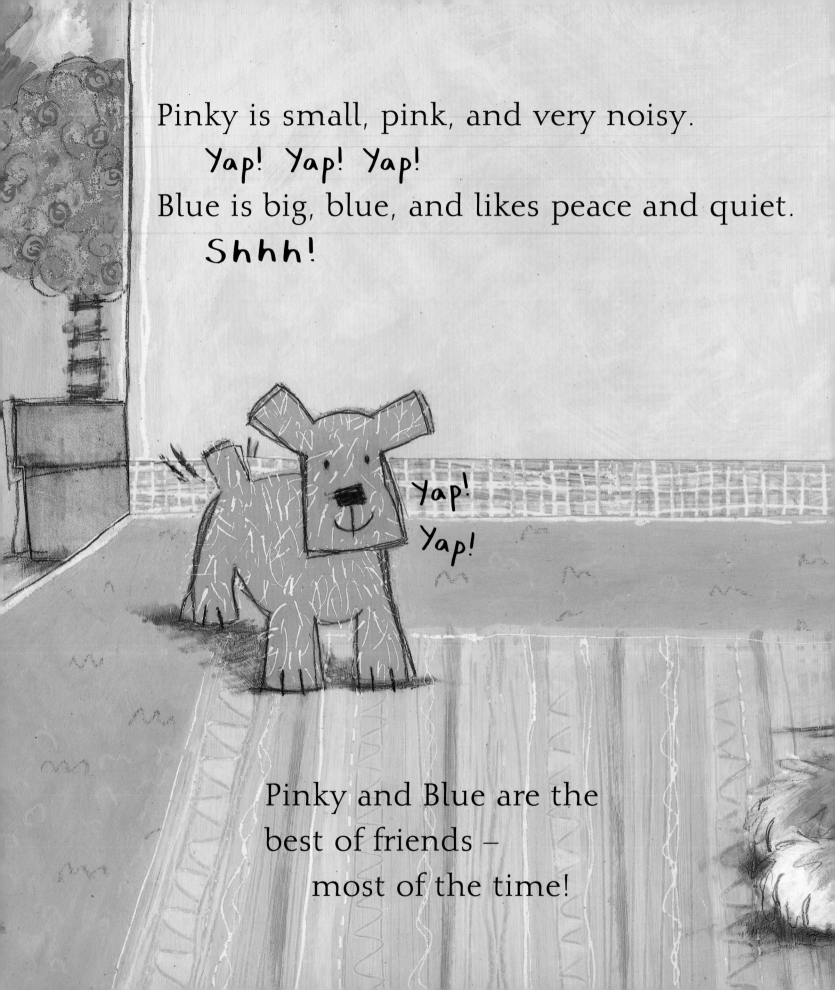

Pinky is small, pink, and very noisy.
Yap! Yap! Yap!
Blue is big, blue, and likes peace and quiet.
Shhh!

Yap!
Yap!

Pinky and Blue are the
best of friends –
most of the time!

They eat together.

But Pinky eats lots...
        sometimes she eats Blue's food too.

Yap!
    Yap!
        Yap!

Oh no, Pinky!

They love to play together.

But Pinky sometimes runs off
with Blue's bouncy ball.

Yap!

Yap!

Yap!

Oh no, Pinky!

They sleep together.
Yawn!
Zzzz!
Snore!
But sometimes
Pinky can't sleep...

Blue likes having Pinky around and she doesn't mind sharing...

her food

(well, not much)

or her bed

or her rubber ball.

But there's just one thing
that Blue does NOT share…

SQUISHY RABBIT!
Pinky wants Squishy Rabbit all for herself.

Pinky and Blue tug and tug –

Push! **Woof!** Pull! Yap!
Push! **Woof!** Pull! Yap!

until...

off comes Squishy Rabbit's ear!
Pinky thinks it's funny...

Oh no, Pinky!

Dog Tales...

Sula

Thud!

but Blue is angry.
  "Go away, Pinky," shouts Blue.
  "You spoil everything!"

And that's what Pinky did.

Plod!

Plod!

Plod!

All the way to the back of the yard.

Poor Pinky felt sad,
all alone in the shed.

She was cold
and it was getting dark.

But Blue was happy.

She didn't have to share her toys,

she didn't have to share her food,

she could sleep peacefully, and best of all...

Blue had Squishy Rabbit all to herself!

But Blue began to miss Pinky.
She missed Pinky's

Yap!

Yap!

Yap!

She missed Pinky tugging at her tail and
she missed having someone to play with.

Blue missed Pinky...

and Pinky missed Blue!

So Pinky decided
to come back.

She climbed
in through
the window.

Clunk!

And Blue was very happy to have her home!

Now Pinky still
eats Blue's food.

Gulp!
Gulp!

Pinky

Blue

She still runs off
with her bouncy ball.

She still tugs at her tail…

Yelp!

and she is still VERY noisy.

Yap!
Yap!
Yap!

And Blue still shares her food.

She still shares her bouncy ball.

She still shares her bed and

she still likes peace and quiet.

Shhh!

Blue

But Pinky tries not to run off
with Squishy Rabbit anymore,
   and Blue tries not to get angry.

This way they get along really well…